The Magic Fairy Godmother

Jessica Hill

Published by Clink Street Publishing 2019

ISBN: 978-1-912850-48-8
ebook: 978-1-912850-49-5

Clink Street

London | New York

For my dear family who have loved and supported me through adversity. You have always been proud of my drive and ambition and desire to succeed.

Once upon a time, there was a puzzling creature named Hesta who lived in the most beautiful castle in the land. Her beauty was hidden and her hands were tied. Everyone, including the wild animals wondered what or who she was. Cries were heard and tears were shed. Sniffles were being noted.

Then, one day a dashing prince, called Lance went past on a beautiful unicorn with a bright, multicolor mane and tail. He stopped when he heard the cries.

"Hey! Hello there! Please stop crying," a sudden yelling of words.

She turned, her long, wavy, flowing hair just catching the wind. She was so taken by him she wanted to leap onto the unicorn, who was called Star.

Lance was blown away by her rare features. He knew he had to help Hesta, so he hopped off Star and climbed over the castle walls to free her. She then jumped onto the unicorn with his help and they galloped off into the distance. "Thank you", she shrieked, a smile almost appearing across her face.

"There is a ball, would you like to come with me?", Lance gushed. "Yes of course," she answered with little hesitation. Disappearing over the horizon they finally stopped. Gazing into each others eyes, they realised their love was blossoming.

Suddenly, the Magic Fairy Godmother appeared.

She waved her magic wand and Hesta turned into the most fabulous, dazzling princess!

Stunned by the change, Lance, the dashing prince also had a new outfit. The Fairy Godmother struck her magic once again and Star was blessed with wings. With excitement the pair thanked her, jumped onto the unicorn and flew to the ball. It was a great success, dancing and laughing, fit for a Prince and Princess.

Just in a flash, the Fairy Godmother disappeared, but before she left, she said to the couple "I have a surprise for you". Hesta feared that her dreams would be over. She would return to that ugly duckling she had felt before.

At midnight, as the sun was setting, Lance and Hesta sealed their love with a kiss. With that, the Magic Fairy Godmother came before their eyes again.

Without saying anything, she struck her wand
and crowned them King and Queen, a life
to finally behold for the trapped beautiful
creature, Hesta.

CPSIA information can be obtained
at www.ICGtesting.com
Printed in the USA
LVHW072300291019
635787LV00015B/223/P